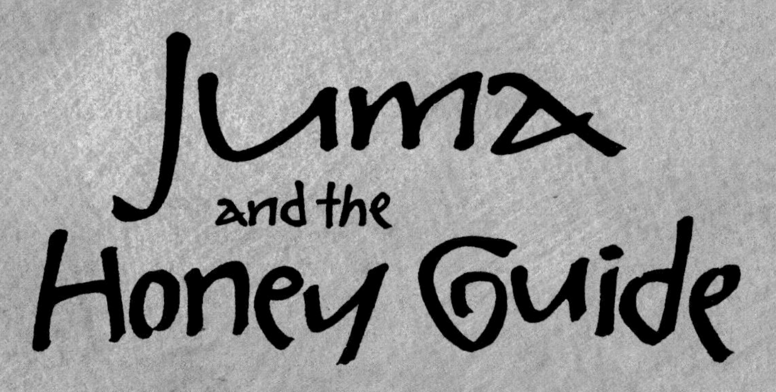

AN AFRICAN STORY

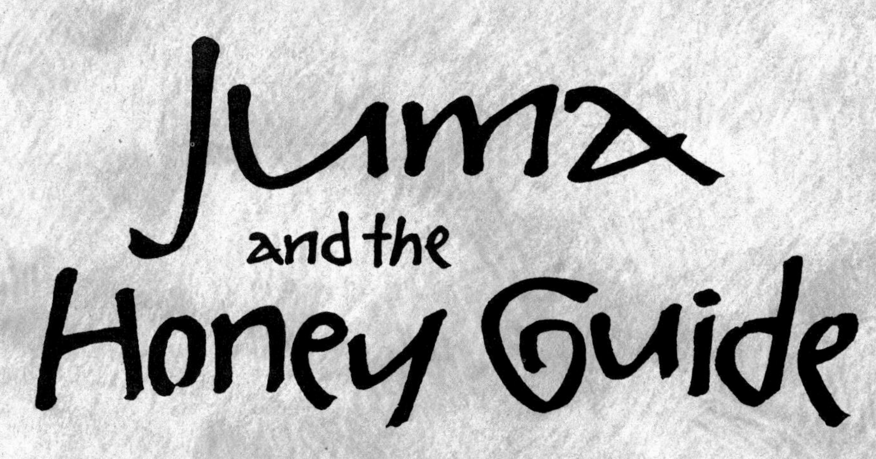

AN AFRICAN STORY

By Robin Bernard

Illustrated by Nneka Bennett

Silver Press
Parsippany, New Jersey

For Jerry. Sasa na sikuzoke. R.B.

To my mother N.B.

Text copyright © 1996 by Robin Bernard
Illustrations copyright © 1996 by Nneka Bennett

All rights reserved including the right of reproduction in whole or in part in any form.

Published by Silver Press
A Division of Simon & Schuster
299 Jefferson Road, Parsippany, NJ 07054

Designed by Studio Goodwin Sturges
Calligraphy by Colleen © 1996

Printed in the United States of America

ISBN 0-382-39162-4 (LSB) 10 9 8 7 6 5 4 3 2 1
ISBN 0-382-39163-2 (JHC) 10 9 8 7 6 5 4 3 2 1
ISBN 0-382-39164-0 (PBK) 10 9 8 7 6 5 4 3 2 1

Library of Congress Cataloging-in-Publication Data
Bernard, Robin,
Juma and the Honey Guide/by Robin Bernard; illustrated by Nneka Bennett. p. cm.
Summary: After teaching his son how to find honey by following the honey-guide bird, an African father insists that they thank the bird by sharing some of the honey with it.
[1. Africa—Fiction. 2. Blacks—Africa—Fiction. 3. Honey—Fiction. 4. Honeyguides —Fiction. 5. Fathers and sons—Fiction.] I. Bennett, Nneka, ill. II. Title.
PZ7.B455135Ju 1996 95-20007
[E]—dc20 CIP
AC

How to say the Swahili words in this story

SWAHILI	ENGLISH
baba (BAH bah)	father
ndio (ihn DEE oh)	yes
kidege (kih DEG ee)	little bird
asante (uh SAHN tay)	thank-you
hapana (huh PAHN uh)	no

"The honey-guide bird is calling to me," Bakari told his son. "I will follow him and bring home a treat."

"May I come with you, Baba?" Juma asked.

"Ndio," Bakari answered, "come, and I will teach you how to get honey."

Juma and his father followed the singing bird out of the village. As they walked through the tall yellow grass, they passed giraffes nibbling the leaves of an umbrella tree, and a pair of ostriches trotting ahead of their fuzzy chicks.

They passed glossy striped zebras and a family of warthogs taking a dust bath.

They passed a rocky outcrop where pygmy mongooses squeaked as they played jump-and-tumble games.

Finally they came to a group of yellow acacia trees beside a waterhole. The honey-guide bird settled on a branch and stopped singing.

"Listen, Juma, and tell me what you hear," Bakari said.

"Only the wind, baba. The kidege is quiet."

"By being quiet," Bakari explained, "he tells us that we are *very* close to the bee's nest. And look! There it is, right in that tree!"

Juma watched his father gather dry twigs and build a small fire at the foot of the tree. Bakari sprinkled water on it so that it made a lot of smoke but hardly any flame.

As the smoke drifted up and into the nest, the bees buzzed angrily and flew away.

Bakari poked the empty nest with his walking stick. He caught it as it fell and held it out to show Juma. "This is a fine one," he said. The honey looks dark and sweet. Try some."

Juma dipped his finger in the comb and licked it off. It was the best honey he ever tasted!

Bakari broke off a chunk and handed it to him. Juma was about to take a bite when his father pointed to the tree and said, "Climb up and leave this piece in the fork of that branch."

Juma was puzzled. He thought the piece was for him. "But why, Baba?" he asked. "There is so much honey in this piece! Why should I leave it on a tree?"

"Because," Bakari explained, "this is how we say asante to the kidege. After all, he found the nest. Then he told us about it, and then he showed us just where to find it, didn't he?"

But Juma didn't want to give up the honeycomb. He thought it was silly to waste good honey on a kidege.

"But Baba," he complained, "why does the kidege need such a big piece? I think we should take it all home."

"That would not be right," Bakari told him. "It would be a selfish thing to do. The kidege would be very angry and make a bad thing happen."

Juma thought of how good the honeycomb would taste on the way home. And wasn't he more important than the kidege? Besides, how could such a tiny bird do anything very bad?

"What kind of bad thing can a kidege do, Baba? Can he sing all night and keep us awake?"

"Hapana," Bakari said, "the kidege cannot keep us awake. Now please put the honeycomb in the tree, Juma."

"Can he drop a lizard into the cookpot and spoil our dinner?"

"Hapana," Bakari said, "the kidege cannot spoil our dinner. Now please put the honeycomb in the tree, Juma."

"Can he poke holes in our roof and let the rain pour in?"

"Hapana, the kidege cannot poke holes in our roof," Bakari said. "Now please put the honeycomb in the tree, Juma."

"But Baba, what kind of bad thing CAN the kidege do?" Juma asked.

Bakari lowered his voice. "Some other time," he said, "the kidege can call to you, and you will follow him thinking of sweet dark honey. But instead of leading you to a bee's nest . . . he can lead you to a hungry LION!"

Juma climbed the tree in a flash. He placed the piece of honeycomb in the fork in the branch.

"Baba," he called, "This looks too small. Maybe we should leave a bigger piece for the kidege!"